BELSHAZZAR, also known as Bell, Belli or Schmelli, was born in England and is the son of the late Nebuchadnezzar. He received his early education under the tutelage of his mother and thereafter was entirely self-taught. Belshazzar was adopted by a British family with whom he lived, except for one brief and unfortunate period of time when he was forced to take up residence elsewhere. This is Belshazzar's first book, and it was accomplished with the assistance of author Chaim Bermant and illustrator Meg Rutherford.

BELSHAZZAR

A Cat's Story For Humans

CHAIM BERMANT

Illustrated by
MEG RUTHERFORD

 A BARD BOOK/PUBLISHED BY AVON BOOKS

Cover illustration by Meg Rutherford

AVON BOOKS
A division of
The Hearst Corporation
959 Eighth Avenue
New York, New York 10019

Text Copyright © 1979 by Chaim Bermant
Illustrations Copyright © 1979 by Meg Rutherford
Published by arrangement with the author and the illustrator
Library of Congress Catalog Card Number: 81-52387
ISBN: 0-380-58560-x

First Bard Printing, May, 1982

BARD TRADEMARK REG. U. S. PAT. OFF. AND IN
OTHER COUNTRIES, MARCA REGISTRADA, HECHO EN
U. S. A.

Printed in the U.S.A.

OP   10   9   8   7   6   5   4   3   2   1

CHAPTER 1

eople often ask me (as if it's any of their business) how I, a
t, came to be called Belshazzar. The answer, to those familiar
ith the Book of Daniel, will, I fear, seem banal. My father (of
essed memory) was called Nebuchadnezzar. I have no idea
hy he was called Nebuchadnezzar, for he was not, as far as I
1ow, Babylonian, but was, if truth be told, a somewhat
:omiscuous Tom with doubtful habits who, while still in the
:ime of life, was rendered inarticulate by an articulated lorry.
I would not have cared to be called Nebuchadnezzar but
do like the name Belshazzar, possibly because I am rather
nd of myself and the name reminds me of me. Moreover, I
:efer it to Felix, or Whiskers or Fluffy or Flopsie or Pussums,
hich we cats have to suffer, and, apart from anything else, it's
good mouthful. Unfortunately, people being what they are,
ey're too lazy to call me by my full name and make do with
ell, or Belli or even Schmelli. Not that I answer to any name
all, unless, of course, there's something I fancy in the
Fing, when they can call me what they please. Otherwise, of
burse, I come and go as I like.
But before I go any further I should perhaps get one rather
delicate fact out of the way. It is not the sort of fact I care
dwell on but people these days rarely dwell on anything
se, and there is no way of avoiding it. I am referring to sex,
:, more particularly my sex, or, rather, the lack of it. One
ould have thought it was a private matter (no pun intended),
something between me and other cats, but no. Every time
e have a visitor he, or more usually she, will chuck me under
ae chin and ask: 'Has he had his operation?' – or has he been
octored, or neutered, or treated (that's the one that gets me,
:reated', as if I'd been taken out to a birthday tea or some-
aing), or the thousand and one other names they have for it,
which I slink away in disgust.
What they, of course, mean is: have I been castrated? And
ae answer is that it is a matter of complete indifference to me –
s it should be to them – whether I have or not, which may

suggest that I have, indeed, been castrated. People tell me tha[t] what you've never had you never miss and certainly to judg[e] from the behaviour of those who do have it – cats and no[n] cats alike – I feel better off without it. To which I might ad[d] even without 'it' (whatever it might be) I still have my admirer[s] for I am, if I say so myself, a handsome creature nicely rigge[d] out with a fine, sleek coat, jet black, except for a white dick[ey] and white spats, all of which I keep spotless.

I wish I could say that my surroundings are in keeping wit[h] my appearance, but they are not. I live in a small suburba[n] house with a garden that is always threatening to revert t[o] jungle, and sometimes does, among people who are no grande[r] than the house and no better kempt than the garden. Needles[s] to say, I hate them all.

There is first of all Zombie, a great, shaggy dolt wh[o] lumbers around the place like a tame buffalo, who laughingl[y] thinks of himself as master of the house and who potter[s] around most of the time in carpet slippers and a ragge[d] cardigan with a cigarette smouldering in his face, doin[g] nothing in particular, though from time to time he pulls hi[s] finger out of his nose for long enough to poke around on [a] typewriter.

He does nothing in the morning, but does it actively. H[e] sleeps in the afternoon with his glasses parked on his forehea[d] and, if he's remembered to put his cigarette out, I settle dow[n] on his lap. Otherwise I sit at his feet to see if he'll catch fir[e] which somehow he never does.

I don't mind him really, except when he stands on me, o[r] catches my tail in the door (for he is the clumsiest creature yo[u] can imagine), but I do mind *her*, the chatelaine of the estab[-] lishment who, for reasons which will become clear later, [I] call Scragends. As I said, I hate them all, but with an ordinar[y] day-to-day passionless hatred, but my hate for her is the rea[l] thing and when I'm weary and listless and do not feel lik[e] stirring even at the sight of a mouse, I need only think of he[r] to come alive. She is small and scraggy, without a bit of mea[t] on her, though how she stays that way I can't think, for sh[e] eats more than the rest of the household put together, includ[ing] ng me, and I can put away a good bit of protein when I get the chance (which, in this particular establishment, isn't often). The kids, and even Zombie, like to leave out little titbits on their plates for me, a bit of fish here, a bit of chicken there, but if she catches them at it there's hell to pay 'They're only scrag-ends, Mummy,' they protest. 'Scrag-ends are food,' she says, and finishes them herself. Hence Scragends. I think she'd swallow arsenic rather than let it go to waste – or to me. Not that she lets me starve. She gives me Pussy Pats, which is about the next best thing. Oh, I've seen some fluffy nit on television going for Pussy Pats as if it was salmon trout. They probably starve the poor creature for a week, or have some rump steak got up to look like Pussy Pats. As for myself, I piss on it (and I don't mean metaphorically), though it does eventually get eaten up, for there are lesser breeds about the place (of whom more later), whose needs are greater than mine and who will eat anything. What I do for my own sustenance is another story. Suffice it to say that I have friends.

If, as I have suggested, Scragends is not particularly free with food, she is a little too free with medicine and rushes me to the vet at the least little thing, as if it was all on the National Health – perhaps she fancies the vet, or maybe she finds medicine cheaper than Pussy Pats. She once had her aged grandmother staying with her and got my medicines mixed up with hers. I don't know what the mix up did to her grandma, but my dicky turned brown for a week. She has four kids (Scragends, I mean, not her grandma) whom I call Brush-in-hand, Pen-in-hand, Son-of-Zombie and Angel-face.

Brush-in-hand (or Brush) is so called because I always see her with a brush in her hand and wouldn't recognise her without one. She's about eleven or twelve, tall and blonde, and fancies herself and spends half her life in front of the mirror brushing her hair this way and that, though whatever she does it usually manages to stay over her eyes and she stumbles around like a badly kempt Afghan hound. I'm supposed to be her cat and like to sleep in her room if I get the chance, but it's such a mess with beds unmade and clothes and books everywhere, a badly strung guitar under the pillow,

half-eaten buns all over the place, to say nothing of the apple-cores, half-sucked toffees, and blobs of bubble gum, that I don't go near it.

Pen-in-hand (or Pen), who I think is nine, is a bit tidier than her sister, but much noisier, jabbering all the time in a loud voice and, as if that isn't bad enough, she fancies herself as something of a pianist and whenever I find myself a nice cosy corner and settle down comfortably with my head between my flanks and my eyes finally closed – bh-wang! She's at the piano. But I call her Pen-in-hand because she's small and black (though she looks blacker than she is because she's usually half-covered in ink) and is nearly always with a pen in hand, drawing, drawing on bits of paper, on her books, on the table-cloth, on the wall – in fact on any flat surface. She once, but only once, tried to draw a black bow-tie on to my pure white dicky, and she still has five broad lines like a music score running down from her wrist to her knuckles to show for it.

Then there's Son-of-Zombie (or Soz), a chip off the old block if ever there was one (poor lad). He once slipped half a kipper into his anorak pocket to pass on to me, but I happened to have been otherwise engaged that day and was not around, and he forgot about it. The weather improved and more than a week passed before he wore the anorak again, by which time the half kipper was making itself felt throughout the house and half-way down the street. Scragends managed to trace the smell to its source, by which time the kipper was a trifle off colour, as was the lad by the time she and Zombie had finished with him.

Finally there is Angel-face (or Angel). Family lore hath it that one of his first actions after sitting up was to sink his chubby little fingers into my side and come away with a handful of fur, and family lore hath it right, for four years after the event he still has a music score (now grown a trifle faint) running down the entire length of his right arm (on which Pen-in-hand once drew in crotchets and played the result on the piano). He's a round little fellow is Angel-face, like a cannonball, and I would cheerfully fire him from a cannon. Instead I do the next best thing. When he's alone in the room and playing quietly, I slink up behind him and then – aargh! I arch my back till every hair is on end, fluff out my tail and hiss, which immediately sends him out shrieking and they come rushing in from all directions.

'It's Bell,' he screams with a quivering finger. 'It's Bell.' But Bell is by then lying there in a corner with a look of puzzled innocence on his face, as if he's just been startled out of his sleep and is anxious to get back into it. I will admit that I sometimes overdo it and after one major trauma there was talk of giving me away or sending me away or even, if I heard it rightly, of putting me away, but I believe that if there had been a choice between getting rid of me and gettting rid of Angel his two sisters and brother would – much as they love him – have voted in my favour.

So much for the fauna within the walls. The fauna without are a trifle more exotic and numerous, and the back garden, which I had regarded initially as my private preserve, is more like a blessed safari park.

There is (there are?) first of all the Persian pair next door, named, if you please, She and Sha, Sha being a he and She a she. They were originally bought for breeding purposes, but either Sha isn't much of a He or She isn't much of a she, and to date they have failed to reproduce, though it isn't for want of trying. The fault, I suspect, lies mainly with She, for a third party and even, I believe, a fourth were (though on different occasions) introduced into the ménage, without effect. She was also treated with a drug so potent that even I nearly made a fool of myself on one occasion and poor old Sha nearly collapsed from his exertions, but still without effect. I have watched their efforts with some sympathy (and not a little amusement) though it would be too much to say that we are friends. There was a time when it was daggers drawn every time we caught sight of each other, and more often than not they got the better of me, partly because there are two of them to one of me, and partly because Persians aren't really cats but walking puff-balls and one is half asphyxiated in fur before one can draw blood. The best thing to do is to go for their

10

ears which are that bit more exposed, and both Sha and She have an ear shorter than the other as a result of our first encounters.

There was quite a to-do about it at the time for they are both show cats and came away with prizes almost every year, but of course, with ears curtailed and bits of fur missing here and there, they did not quite look their best, and their owners (insofar as a cat may be said to have owners – I rather think of them as servants), a long-haired, weedy pair of indeterminate sex (a bit like their cats, I suppose), blamed Clarence. Well everybody blames Clarence for everything and more often than not they're right because although he always means well (or I think he does) when he's around unfortunate things happen, more often than not to himself. He is in fact a huge, black, stupid mut of a dog – in a way he reminds me of Zombie, who wouldn't hurt a fly – and will have a go at anything on four legs, including chairs, tables, park benches, swings and, in moments of utter desperation, other dogs. He even came near to trying me once and still has a scar on his stupid snout to remind him not to try again. Of all the creatures who on earth do dwell he is probably the one I loathe least and, if not quite a friend, he is emphatically a non-enemy.

The same cannot be said for Puffer, a squirrel. I used to think that squirrels hibernate. Well Puffer doesn't, and I don't think he sleeps either, and he's up to mischief at any time of the year and at most times of the day or night, mischief, I may add, for which I usually get blamed. If you can imagine a piglet with a fluffy tail and a grey fur coat, then you've got something like Puffer, who is always stealing and always eating, and hence rather fat and breathless (whence the name Puffer), but he's as quick as the wind. I have tried to catch him often enough, so have Sha and She, so has Clarence, but whenever you get near him he smartly folds his tail back against his neck and whoosh! – he's gone.

Clarence lives with an old man who was abandoned by his wife years ago and who hardly eats anything himself (though he makes up for it in drink) and more or less leaves Clarence to live off the land. Scragends has a soft spot for Clarence and she leaves out bits and pieces for him which I wouldn't mind nibbling myself, but, as soon as her back is turned, Puffer – if he's not busy elsewhere – whips in and whips off and leaves the poor doggie with none, and many a day he has to make do with my Pussy Pats, which is a fate I wouldn't wish on a dog.

Then there is Spike, a hedgehog with the sort of personal habits which give hogs of any variety a bad name. He steals, as does Puffer, but Puffer makes a clean job of it, and tries not to be seen. Spike merely waits for darkness then trots up to help himself to anything that's going, which usually happens to be the bowl of milk put out for me in the back garden or garage. Brush, Pen and the others usually see to it that I get a

fairly generous helping and there is usually some to spare after I've finished, only Spike doesn't wait that long but sidles up, sniffing and grunting, thrusts his long snout forward and helps himself, at which, of course, I give up. But that is not the limit of his chutzpah. He has a habit, when drinking out of a bowl, of climbing right into the wretched thing, and, so to speak, having a meal and a bath in one. I daren't go near him because, apart from the prickles, every time he moves he sends up a cloud of fleas. Clarence came charging down upon him one night, snarling and barking, but Spike merely lifted up a leg and farted in his face, and continued with his meal, sniggering quietly to himself.

There isn't a dog or a cat for miles around whose food he doesn't raid, always leaving a small cluster of dead fleas round the rim of the bowl as a memento of his visit. He's afraid of no one – no one, that is, except the one that everyone's afraid of, Genghis, known also as the Yellow Menace. Genghis's father, they say, was a promiscuous ginger tom, but he himself is more like a cross between a hyena and an alligator, for he's as long and as low as the one and as vicious as the other, and those who have been near him say he has webbed feet, which I doubt, for he's afraid of water. He is certainly bigger than any cat I've ever seen and can, when in a fury, inflate himself to about twice his size.

We always get good warning of his approach for he stinks like a sewer: even Spike is perfumed by comparison. And then you can hear the birds twittering loudly and rising excitedly from the bushes and trees as he draws near, and suddenly shooting into the sky. At such times you don't stop to think what a lovely meal they might make, but dive for cover like everyone else – all a trifle undignified, you might think, but there are moments in life when even a cat has no time for dignity.

There is a little brook running along the bottom of our garden, which runs parallel to the street and separates our garden from the gardens backing on to ours. It sometimes overflows in the early spring and causes a bit of flooding but otherwise it's hardly more than a trickle. It was, however, enough to keep Genghis out of our parish, until a pair of asses took it upon themselves to build a small bridge linking their two gardens, and life hasn't been quite the same since. The first we knew of Genghis was when he climbed into a house two doors away, bit through a bird-cage and swallowed the parrot, beak and all. His owners, or at least the owners of the property he chooses to grace with his presence, two dear white haired old ladies, denied he could have been responsible, even though he kept coughing up coloured feathers.

'No, not Genghis, never him,' said one.

'He's far too gentle,' said the other.

'He's afraid of parrots.'

'Especially talking parrots.'

'They can be so rude.'

'And they've such sharp beaks.'

'He wouldn't go near them.'

'Not parrots.'

'And besides,' they added in chorus, 'we've brought him up as a vegetarian.'

As a matter of fact I was brought up to eat kosher (though I don't think I'm expected to wait three hours between meat and milk), but I do fancy a bit of bird on the wing, which, in case you didn't know it, is non-kosher. Older birds are wary of my approach, but each spring there is a new generation who don't know about cats, or anything else for that matter, and who peck around unsuspectingly in the grass till – wham! I pounce. I don't do a Genghis, which is to say I don't swallow them whole, which is in any case a wasteful thing to do. I just sort of wing them and then let them hop around until I'm ready for my meal. The kids once found a thrush whom I had knocked about a bit, and they tried to feed and water it, and when it wouldn't touch food or water they took it to the vet to see if he could do anything for it, but all he could do was to put it away, and I had to keep out of their way for a day or two after that. Son-of-Zombie, usually my most generous benefactor, threw a stone at me (he missed of course) and said I was nasty and cruel and asked what pleasure did I get out of harming a poor little bird.

'He goes after birds because he likes to eat them,' explained Brush-in-hand.

'But they're not kosher,' said Son-of-Zombie incredulously.

Then Pen-in-hand read somewhere that cats only go after birds when they're hungry, and even persuaded Scragends of this fact, and for about a week after that every meal was a banquet, but there is, of course, nothing to compare with a nice tender fledgling. One spring morning, after the kids had fed me a hearty breakfast, they came out into the garden and found me with a young blackbird still twitching and twittering between my jaws. They immediately gave chase and I dived through the hedge into the garden next door, shot over the bridge and ran full-tilt into Genghis. I dropped the bird at his feet as a peace-offering, but he wasn't hungry and he went after me instead. I am rather lighter on my feet than he is and before I knew what I was doing I found myself in the uppermost branches of a hawthorn tree, with Genghis doing a war-dance round the bottom, and I had the choice between being prickled to death by the hawthorns and being torn apart by Genghis. As a matter of fact it wasn't much of a choice for when I tried to climb down I couldn't. They had to call the fire brigade, who seemed to be in no hurry to get there, and it was nearly dark before I got down and no one seemed to be in a hurry to comfort me or feed me even then, though Scragends put out a bowl of Pussy Pats which I ate hungrily.

'He's wicked, you shouldn't give him anything,' said Son-of-Zombie.

'Cats are cats,' said Scragends, and for a moment I almost ceased to hate her.

CHAPTER 2

One wintry afternoon I was – or thought I was – alone at home and was sitting on the staircase landing, half awake, half asleep, watching the day grow darker through the glass panel of the front door. I like the staircase landing partly because it gives a good view of the street outside and partly because even in winter – especially in winter – it is about the warmest place in the house, for it is well carpeted and padded with underfelt, and it gets any sunshine and warmth that is going, and keeps it long after the sun has gone down.

Anyway, as I said, I was sitting there half asleep, half awake when I heard something stir in an upstairs room. I should have gone to investigate but I was too comfortable and too sleepy and too lazy and remained where I was in the gathering dusk. Then a door opened and I recognised the footsteps of a stout party, an elderly relative or maybe lodger, called Dr

Kuchel, who stayed with them from time to time. He was a short breathless man with thick glasses and wore a black beret, a grubby sheepskin coat several times too large for him, and heavy boots. I should have got out of his way when I heard his tread but I thought he would have noticed a full-grown cat even in the twilight. He didn't and stomped right on top of me. I gave a yell and jumped in the air. So did he, then he fell headlong down the stairs and landed with a thud against the wall, his glasses shattered. I sat there petrified for a minute, not quite sure what had happened, but then when he didn't stir I gingerly came down the stairs, stepping carefully amidst the broken glass, walked round him in a circle for a bit, came nearer, sniffed him over and then, satisfied that he was quite inert, I settled on the broad lapel of his sheepskin coat and fell asleep.

I don't know how long I had slept when I was awakened by a sharp whack across the ears. Now I don't care to be roused from my sleep at the best of times, especially with a sharp whack across the ears, but I could see as I half opened my eyes that I had occasioned some sort of displeasure. Zombie was bending down over the stout party, Scragends was speaking hurriedly into the telephone and the children were standing round in a circle, their hands to their cheeks, their faces aghast. Clearly they thought that I had had something to do with the commotion, which in a way I had, though as a matter of fact I was the injured party rather than the injuring one. Who had stomped on whom in the first place? If a man can't walk down a staircase without stomping on a full-grown cat he shouldn't be allowed out on his own, but I wouldn't expect them to understand that and I slunk away in case they should inflict further injury. In any case I was hungry. I went into the kitchen but nobody had put out any milk for me. I went to the garage (in which they kept everything but their car) but found not a thing – not even Pussy Pats, though at that particular moment I was hungry enough to eat even them (the cold weather does give one an appetite, does it not?) and I went down the road to the Ancients, an elderly, derelict pair, who look as if they live on bread and water themselves, and probably do, but fill their house with choice morsels – fish, chicken, liver, chicken-liver, gold-top milk slightly warmed – for my delectation. Theirs is also the only house in the street with an open fire, and as they feel the cold even in summer (on those occasions when there is a summer) they have coals blazing all the year round, which makes it sound like paradise and which, in a way, it is, except that the old woman keeps chucking me around the chin and the ears, and brushing me and combing me, and stroking me, and pulling me on to her lap and talking to me, and clucking to me as if I was a chicken, so that I sometimes feel I'm better off with the cold rooms and Pussy Pats of the other place. Moreover, one day when I was asleep on the hearth-rug, a piece of blazing coal bounced out of the fire and landed on my flank.

'Can you smell something burning, m'dear?' says he to her.

By the time I had jumped to my feet it had burned a hole the size of a ten pence piece. Well, it's nearly repaired now, but I haven't used their hearth-rug since. And I can't use their fireside chairs either, for I'm no sooner settled or asleep than one or the other of them sits on me. She's as light as a feather, so there's not much harm there, but he's not only half blind, but half gaga, and weighs a ton. The fire was crackling one cold afternoon and I was dozing merrily when he plonks his great big bottom on top of me and stifles me so completely that I can hardly let out a squawk and all I can do is struggle for sweet life with all the strength I have left.

'You know,' he says to her, 'the chairs need re-doing.'

'Re-doing, m'dear,' she says. 'They've just been re-done.'

'Re-done were they?'

'Yes dear, only last week.'

'Well the springs in this one play up no end.'

I once inveigled Spike into climbing into his chair and while he was snuffling around poking his snout into the corners the old boy comes shuffling in and splat! Sits right on top of him. I thought he'd be up again in a flash, but he must have been made of leather and if Spike hadn't managed to work his way into a corner and then out through the stuffing that would have been the end of him. As it was, it was the end of the chair.

All that, however, was in the past and all I had my mind on at the moment was the thought of the glowing fire, the fresh liver and the warm milk. But when I got to the house I stopped short. The place was in darkness, the doors were bolted. There wasn't anything in the tray by the back door which she sometimes left out for me; there wasn't even the tray. Old people do have a nasty habit of dropping dead without warning and without notice. Could that have happened to them, and both on the same day? I tried every opening, doors and windows; I even clambered on to the icy roof to try the skylights, but they too were closed. I sat huddled against the cold chimney-top wondering what to do next and decided that there was nothing for it but to go back, which was easier said than done for to shin up a roof (if you're a cat) or a tree or a drainpipe is one thing, to get down is quite another. Every time I reached out I found myself slithering, and quickly pulled myself back to my perch by the chimney. I turned this way and that and it grew so cold that I thought I'd be frozen to the tiles. Then, as I was trying to make my way towards the side of the house where I thought I might be able to climb down the ivy, I lost my grip, shot down the tiles and landed with a thump in the gutter and would have come crashing down but for the fact that I was able to hold on by my front claws, with the rest of me dancing and twitching, kicking out wildly to grip at something but gripping only the cold night air. Then, still dangling, I tried to work my way along claw over claw to the corner, but the gutter began to give way, at first slowly with a creaking noise, and then with a sharp crack and I plummeted straight into a rose bush. This, said I, as I was flailing the air with all fours, is not my day. Cats may always land on their feet, but that does not mean to say that falling from a roof is a pleasure.

When I got back home the children were in bed but I knew as soon as I showed my face in the kitchen that I had been the topic of conversation, and that I had been spoken of with less than affection, and I beat a hasty retreat to the garage where I found some two-day-old Pussy Pats and ate them as if they were salmon trout.

The next day Pen-in-hand addressed me in stern tones. 'You're a wicked pussy,' she said: 'you nearly killed poor, dear Dr Kuchel.'

Nearly killed him? So what was all the fuss about? I thought I *had* killed him.

'It was bad enough sitting on the stairs when Mummy warned you ever so often not to,' she went on. 'That's how he tripped over and fell – but it was worse sitting on top of him with your bottom right up against his mouth. You might have stifled him, besides it's unhygienic.'

'If you do that again they'll send you away,' said Son-of-Zombie.

'They'll not send you away,' said Brush-in-hand, 'they'll *put* you away,' but as they had all saved me some small titbits from their breakfast I didn't mind the admonition. Scragends and Zombie said nothing, but I was by now sensitive enough to situations to understand that I was on probation.

A month or two or perhaps six months (cats have no sense of time) later and it was Passover, a time of the year when they turn the house inside out and when – if you keep your wits about you – you may encounter small, furry, scurrying mice, which are fun to catch (if you can catch them) and delectable when caught. There is also more food about the house – though I am told the whole occasion is meant to recall a time of privation and hardship in Egypt – and finally they don't permit the usual tinned foods, – including Pussy Pats, about the place, and for a glorious eight days I am kept on real food, which is to say fish, flesh and good red herring.

Well, one day I was out in the gardens (I use the plural because I move fairly freely from one to the other, now through bush, now through briar, and occasionally even through gate) when I saw something furry darting about. It was too long for a mouse and too short for a squirrel, and besides its tail wasn't fluffy. I lay low and then, almost moving on my stomach, crept nearer. It was scratching away at something too busy to see and hear. Then, slowly coiling myself up, I pounced. It was a bit larger than I thought, and a good deal stronger, but I soon had it under control and I carried it away, still twitching between my jaws, to a quiet corner where I could enjoy it in peace, but as I turned a corner I ran full tilt into Genghis. This time, however, I did not drop my quarry at his feet as a peace-offering – I'd had to fight too hard to get it – but turned sharply at right angles and dived through a bush. He dived after me, then through another, then a third, where I lost him for a while, though I knew he couldn't be far behind, and I dashed to the garage. My idea was to hide the rat where he couldn't reach it and as I was looking around for a likely place I noticed something new at the far end of the garage, rather like a very narrow bath. I jumped up to have a look and found it half full of chickens, joints, fish, all covered in plastic and all frozen stiff. It was, on reflection, a silly thing to do, but without another thought I jumped with my mouthful into the box and as I did so the lid slammed shut on top of me.

I turned feverishly in all directions. I scratched, I howled,

but without effect. My voice grew weaker, my strength was giving out. I was frightened, I couldn't breathe. I was turning to ice.

I'm not sure if cats do or do not have nine lives – arithmetic was never my strong point – but if they do I had lost eight of them by the time the box was opened. I caught a momentary glimpse of Scragends before she slammed it shut with a loud scream. It was opened again a minute later by Zombie, who stood there staring open-mouthed. I must have made a pretty picture for I was covered with white frost like fine silver dust, and there were tiny icicles at the tips of my whiskers which sagged down on both sides of my mouth, but that was probably not how Zombie saw me. On reflection I must have looked like a Christmas decoration. I just had enough strength to crawl out, to crawl down and to shuffle into the corner by the boiler to thaw out. I didn't know what they would do to me, and I didn't care.

But there was quite a to-do for, although it had slipped my mind, the rat was still in the freezer, in a pool of frozen blood. I had also, in my struggles to get out, torn the plastic covering on a twelve pound turkey, a full-grown salmon and half a cow, and they too were covered with blood. (I never knew one middle-sized rat could have so much blood.) They weren't pleased about it for the trouble with rats is you never know where they've been. They're not kosher, they're not *pesach-dick* (you couldn't eat them, or anything with which they've come into contact, during Passover), and if it comes to that they're not particularly hygienic, and they had to throw out the entire contents of the freezer. There was even talk about whether they should keep the freezer or not. There was no talk about whether they should keep me; that was settled the moment Scragends opened the freezer. Nobody seemed put out by the thought that I nearly died a triple death of fright, asphyxiation and cold in that wretched box. People have no right keeping an open freezer in the house when they have domestic pets, or, indeed, undomestic ones.

Scragends was ill upstairs and Zombie told the kids of the mishap when they came home from school. 'He's a menace, he's driving us all round the bend and he'll have to go,' he said.

Two voices were raised in defence.

'It's not his fault, he's only a cat you know,' said Son-of-Zombie.

'He's only a cat, you know,' echoed Angel-face.

'I don't care if he's a canary. He's a dangerous nuisance, and if there'd have been a stream handy I'd have drowned him.' At which they all drew in their breath.

'You wouldn't drown Bell,' they all said aghast.

'I would and I will if he does anything like this again, only he won't for he's going.'

'Can't he have one, just one more chance?' pleaded Pen.

'He's had too many chances. Can't you see he's a menace. Have you forgotten how he nearly killed Dr Kuchel – and now he puts a bleeding rat in the freezer.'

Would it have been better, I wondered, if I had nearly killed a rat and put Dr Kuchel in the freezer?

They all went to bed in tears that night. I can't say I was too happy myself, especially as I hadn't quite thawed out. There was nothing I could do to keep warm, and they hadn't put out any food for me, not even Pussy Pats. I wasn't at all sure that I would survive the night, but, dead or alive, one thing was certain: my days *chez* Zombie were numbered. I could see the writing on the wall – and who better?

CHAPTER 3

They say a cat always lands on its feet and I certainly did that time.

Brush, after a sleepless night, dressed early and went round to see the Old Pair, who hardly sleep at all, or, rather, are hardly awake at all, for they doze off at all hours, but are always up and about at the crack of dawn. Anyway, she sat down in the kitchen with them and over a hot cup of tea told them all that had befallen – or rather into what I had fallen – the day before.

'Poor pussy,' said the Old Girl, 'poor pussy,' and she shuffled over to the fridge to prepare me a nice bit of whiting. 'Has he got over it, poor thing?'

'He has but Daddy hasn't,' said Brush, 'and he'll have to leave.'

'Who, your dad?'

'No, the cat.'

'The cat?'

'Yes, Daddy won't put up with him any more.'

'Then he'll have to come here – won't he, Eric?'

'What's that, Rita?'

'I said he'll have to come here.'

'Yes, you can tell your dad he can stop here.'

Anyway, to cut a long story short I was transferred with all my possessions, including my basket and maybe two years' supply of Pussy Pats (I think Scragends bought them whole-sale).

I should have been in clover, well I was in clover, but I should have been happy about it and I wasn't, not at first. You know how it is, you get used to what you're used to, old haunts, old smells, old nooks and crannies, old routines – perhaps even old discomforts – and I missed Brush and Pen and the others; I even began to miss Scragends (the fact that I also hated them is beside the point), but in time I got used to the change. Brush, Pen and the others came round every day, sometimes several times a day, leaning over the garden gate on

the way to school, and then on the way from school, and then Son-of-Zombie would be around with something he'd saved me from his tea – not that I was in need of it, living as I was off (or is it on?) the fat of the land, but a cat can always find room for a little more. Clarence also discovered my new billet, as did Puffer and Spike with his attendant retinue of fleas, so that it was almost like old times, only better. The one fly in the ointment was Genghis, who lived almost within whiffing distance, so that I was nearly always aware of him even if I couldn't see him.

Another fly in the ointment was the fact that there was no 'pussy-panel' to the kitchen door, so that I had to attract their attention whenever I wanted to come and go, which wasn't all that easy, for they were both half deaf and there were times when I nearly burst before I could nip out to my favourite corner of the garden to do what has to be done.

The third fly (if I go on at this rate there'll be more flies than ointment) is that the Old Pair did not keep the sabbath. Let me explain.

In the other place most days had their quota of harassments, but the sabbath was restful. The house was warmer, the fare was better and all was quiet. The piano was still, the radio and television were off, even the telephone was silent, and they would sit in the lounge (which was about the only time of the week on which the room was in use) and talk quietly or not at all. Zombie would settle in an armchair and drop off; Scrag-ends would read, and so would the others (though Angel-face could be a bit of a nuisance). I liked the restful, untramelled, cosiness of the day. Not that the Old Pair were restless, but they were noisy, for they addressed one another in loud voices, and the Old Girl couldn't switch on the television without offering a running commentary on what she saw, which went something like this.

She: 'She's lovely, isn't she?'

He: 'She's what?'

She: 'Lovely.'

He: 'Yes, she is, isn't she?'

She: 'Always the same hat, haven't you noticed?'

29

He: 'Always.'

She: 'A nice hat, but it's always the same – or at least it always looks the same.'

He: 'Don't suppose she can afford another, the price things are.'

She: 'Of course she can Eric, that's the Queen Mother.'

He: 'The who?'

She: 'The Queen Mother.'

He: 'The Queen Mother?'

She: 'Yes.'

He: 'I thought I'd seen her somewhere.'

She: 'She's lovely isn't she, bless her.'

He: 'She's what?'

She: 'Lovely.'

And so on. You get tired of it when it goes on for four or five hours at a time, especially when you're trying to sleep – which is what I'm trying to do most of the time.

Also in the other place, when no one was looking, I'd sometimes nip upstairs to the kids' rooms and settle on their beds after they were tucked in and asleep. Lovely and warm, kids' beds are, with a soft fragrance about them. There was nothing lovely or fragrant about the Old Pair's room, except the curtains and bedspreads which were made of a flowery chintz, but the beds themselves were hard, with a musty smell, and lying on top of Rita or Eric was like lying on a pile of old bones. I was also put off by the photo of a nasty-faced harridan which stood on a bedside table and the two glassfuls of dentures which snarled at me in the darkness, but the photo was even more off-putting than the dentures. I couldn't understand how anyone with a face like that would want to be photographed, or why anyone should want to keep a photo of a face like that, especially by their bedside. I'd sooner have had a photo of Genghis by my bedside. In fact if Genghis was a woman he'd probably have looked like that.

Yet another fly in the ointment was the fact that Rita had decided that I was a prize cat and I was always being entered for shows. Well, if I may be so immodest as to say so, I *am* a prize cat, but do not much care for cat shows, as they tend to be full of other cats, and I do not care much for other cats, especially other prize cats. Being a prize cat also meant that I was always being brushed and combed, and it doesn't take much to rub me up the wrong way, especially when Eric, who is so short-sighted that he doesn't know one end of a cat from the other, is doing the brushing, but all that being said I was fairly happy in my new lodgings, insofar as a cat may be said to be happy, which did not, however, mean that I had nothing to grumble about.

It was summer now. It hailed, it stormed, it rained. The days were cold and the nights were colder but their cottage was lovely and snug, especially the kitchen, and sometimes when eating a bit of liver or fish I'd look up from my bowl and there would be Clarence or Puffer or Spike shivering outside, with nose pressed against the window. It was a good life, even though I put on a bit of weight and didn't manage to nip through hedges as nimbly as I used to. I could still get through them, but it was rather like putting on a rough-sided, tight-fitting corset and I often asked myself what would happen if I was to come face to face with Genghis. Some weeks later I found the answer. It was autumn by then and the days were getting shorter and the nights longer and I was having a stroll slightly beyond my parish when suddenly he was there in front of me, large as life and twice as smelly. I didn't about turn, for that would have been fatal. I merely slackened my pace, almost imperceptibly, and continued onwards right past him, as if he wasn't there, and then when I had turned a corner I shot off like a bullet. He followed me. I dived into a hedge, and although the front half of me got through, the back, more substantial, half, did not. I struggled frantically to extricate myself, but the more I struggled the faster I stuck, and if Genghis had caught me in that position I'd be left without a rump – or worse. But, as he raced towards me, She and Sha appeared, looking like patches of heavy mist in the gathering dusk. He stopped in his tracks, looked for a moment from one to the other and somehow managed to attack them both at once (he was long enough for that). Their mistress, shrieking loudly, tried to pull him away, and was pulled in herself, while

31

her husband – a little ungallantly – kept his distance, but called the police, the fire brigade and an ambulance. All three arrived within minutes, by which time, however, She and Sha were without fur and their mistress was virtually without clothes. I, in the meantime, moved quietly backwards out of the hedge and trotted home through the dying day and the flying fur, making a mental note to go on a crash slimming course in case of future emergencies. Such resolutions are easier made than kept, for I can resist anything except food, and I began to notice, as I was performing my ablutions, that it took me longer and longer to give myself a once-over, and the effort was becoming more and more strenuous, and Angel-face observed on one of his visits that I looked like a furry pig. The Old Girl, however, liked me that way. 'Oh,' she would exclaim, 'look at the size of him, isn't he lovely!'

It was winter by now. They had bought a wire fireguard and I was able to luxuriate in front of the open fire, stirring occasionally to wash my smalls or to scratch behind the ear, but otherwise dozing the days away in peaceful bliss. That's the life.

One day the Old Girl slipped on her newly polished floor and broke a leg or something and was confined upstairs in bed. I wasn't around at the time but the first I knew of it was when I found that my milk had not been heated to the right temperature. In fact it had not been heated at all. Then the open fire was allowed to die out without being relit. Eric was apologetic. 'I can't bend down you see, and if I do, I can't straighten up.' The house wasn't exactly cold, but if you're used to a warm, blazing fire, no other form of heating is satisfactory. The Old Girl grew worse, as did the weather. Eric couldn't stir out and various neighbours – including Scragends – came in to help with the shopping. And what do you think she bought? Right first time – Pussy Pats. Also doctors and nurses kept coming and going and an atmosphere of ether and gloom settled on the place which I found asphyxiating.

One evening I was fast asleep in an armchair, enjoying a delicious dream, when a rude hand grasped me by the scruff of the neck and threw me with a thud to the floor. I looked up and saw a thoroughly unpleasant but vaguely familiar face. I searched my memory the whole evening, and then suddenly it clicked. It was the harridan whose photo stood by Rita's bedside table, except that in real life she looked even worse than in the photo.

She had jet-black hair which looked as if it had been dyed, small eyes, red or, rather, flushed cheeks, and a mean mouth. She could have been Genghis's mother.

'It's me daughter,' said Eric. 'She's come to help out. I don't think she cares for cats.' She didn't look as if she cared for anything and I didn't discover the true meaning of hate till I set eyes on her. My feelings for Scragends and the others, by comparison, were ones of gushing affection. My weight problem soon vanished, partly because one could lose weight merely by looking at her, and partly because I was starved. My milk bowl was left unfilled; my foodtray was left empty. After a day or two of this she relented sufficiently to pass on

33

anything left from breakfast or dinner (they didn't appear to eat lunch).

Well, the only thing left from breakfast was rancid bacon rind, which, hungry as I was, I wouldn't touch, and Eric told her I wouldn't touch it.

'Why not?' she demanded.
'Because he's kosher.'
'He's what?'
'He's Jewish.'
'Jewish?'
'He comes from a Jewish home. They don't eat bacon, Jews.'
'He will if he's hungry.'
It never came to the test because when she wasn't looking Eric threw out the bacon, cleaned out the bowl and gave me a bit of sardine, or something like that. It wasn't much, but it was enough to keep body and soul together, especially as Son-of-Zombie, Angel-face and the others remembered me in their meals. My coat lost its sheen: but if it was any consolation

experienced less difficulty in washing myself. I was also banished to the garage, which didn't worry me while the weather was mild, but which became thoroughly unpleasant with the approach of winter, for, unlike the garage in the other place, it wasn't heated. And the winter was the longest, the coldest and cruellest in feline memory.

One morning after a heavy fall of snow, I saw a large, black crow, about the size of a hen, pecking at something in the back garden. I crept slowly towards it. The snow came over my ears and obscured my vision, but it also obscured my movements. Then, as I was preparing to leap, the ground gave way under me. I was on top of the snow-covered, frozen-over garden pond, and fell right through. The crow turned its head and gave me a nonchalant glance before continuing with its meal, while I struggled for dear life. By the time I got out and crept into the shelter of the garage I was almost encased in ice, and I settled into a corner half expecting, half hoping to die of cold and misery. As I was sitting there hugging myself, trying to extract what comfort and warmth there was from the spare tyre of a car, I became aware of a commotion in the house and a noise outside. Cold and wretched though I was I went round to investigate and found a large, white ambulance drawn up by the front gate, and a minute or two later two men appeared with a stretcher and the Old Girl on it, her face as white as the ambulance.

I didn't give her much chance of recovery, not with the way she looked and the age she was, and I crawled back to the garage hoping that I might expire with her. As I said, I don't know if a cat has nine lives, but at that moment I felt that it had at least eight too many.

Well, I recovered, but what was rather more surprising, so did the Old Girl. She came back from hospital if not as right as rain at least on her own two feet, and after about a week the Harridan left, and as soon as she was out of the house the snows melted, the spring came, and my basket was moved from the garage to the kitchen. There was no more rancid bacon rind in my bowl and it was back to fish and flesh and warm milk and cosy naps by the open fire. Brush, Pen and the

others, who were hesitant about coming round while the Harridan was about, were in the house almost every day. Clarence and Puffer showed their faces every now and again, as did Spike and his flea circus. It was like old times again, only all the sweeter for having been written off, and as if to ensure that nothing should impair my tranquillity, Rita stopped her running commentaries on everything seen on TV. In fact she adopted my habit of dropping off to sleep almost as soon as she was settled comfortably in a chair, and sometimes, when she had a travel rug round her, I'd settle on her lap, and we'd both drop off together, warmth against warmth, with her long, thin hand gently stroking my fur.

One evening I awoke, conscious of a weight pressing heavily on top of me. It was her hand, which was cold and clammy. I pulled myself free and it flopped into her lap. It had turned pale green, about the colour of the upholstery.

Eric shuffled in at that moment.

'It's all ready,' he announced. She didn't answer and he came over and shook her gently by the shoulder.

'Rita dear, the cocoa's all ready.' She still didn't reply. 'Doesn't look too good, does she?' he said to me. She didn't. He phoned the doctor and it seemed like days before he came. In the meantime the fire died out, and it was freezing. Eric went upstairs and brought down some blankets and quilts.

'Doesn't look too good at all,' he said, as he tried to make her warm, 'and the cocoa's getting cold.' It wasn't getting half as cold as I was.

The doctor eventually arrived in a heavy, leather, fur-lined coat, held the Old Girl's hand for a moment and said: 'That's it then, I'm afraid.'

'That's what?' said Eric.

'She's dead, poor dear.'

'She can't be dead, she's only been out of hospital a week.'

'But she is, I'm afraid.'

'You're sure she's not just having a nap.'

'I'm quite sure.'

'That is upsetting.'

CHAPTER 4

It was a small funeral, but then she was a small woman and she was taken away in what seemed a rather smallish coffin. Everyone was in tears, except her own daughter. Eric, who had been rather a large man, seemed suddenly shrivelled and dried up and bewildered.

The new order began the day after the funeral. I was moved back to the garage, and it was again rancid bacon rind in my bowl. Son-of-Zombie appeared by the garden gate flourishing something appetising in a plastic bag (the better half of a kipper in fact) but the Harridan chased him away.

'If I catch you dropping rubbish in my back garden, I'll call the police,' she screamed. I liked the '*my* back garden,' as if it was hers, but Eric was good to me and he kept bringing me titbits if he remembered. Sometimes he forgot, or was away, or was ill, and at such times I kept trotting back hopefully to the garage to see if there was anything there, but there wasn't.

If the new order was bad for me, it was even worse for the old man. He liked to doze off in front of the television and then wake about eleven o'clock, make himself cocoa and go to bed, but the late-night television stopped because it was bad for his eyes, she said, and the cocoa stopped too, because it was bad for his digestion.

'Bad for me digestion?' he said.

'Bad for your digestion.'

'I've been taking it for forty years, so did your mum.'

'Mum's dead, and if you keep on taking it you'll be dead yourself.'

Well I suppose that there was a certain logic in that and he didn't argue further, but prohibitions make us all furtive and he would make cocoa when she wasn't looking and smuggle it to bed in his hot-water bottle. He gave me some once; it was not cocoa at its best.

One day when she was out of town and it was perhaps his birthday, or maybe he thought it was mine, he pulled a whole

trout out of the fridge and gave it to me. I was half afraid to
eat it, for I knew there'd be hell to pay, and there was. She
stormed and raved a whole evening, sent him to bed without

supper, for he got up in the middle of the night and with a
torch in hand tried to fry himself a couple of eggs. The torch
battery was on its last legs and he couldn't see what he was
doing. The fat ignited and he dropped the pan with a clang,
and for a minute it looked as if the kitchen might catch fire,
but the Harridan flew down, and doused the flames with a wet
towel, and for a moment stood there with the towel in her
hand looking as if she might be ready to douse him as well.

'You'll be the death of me yet,' she screamed. If only he had
been.

A few weeks later I noticed she had a visitor, a heavily-built
man with a red face, pock-marked neck and a bald head. He
came after the old man was in bed, stayed the night and left in
the early hours of the morning. There were a lot of bottles on

the table when he was around, and her voice seemed to soften.
They did not make a beautiful pair, but it came as a surprise
to me that she had sufficient warmth for that sort of relation-
ship, or to attract a man in the first place. I wished he would
come more often. My wish was to be fulfilled more quickly
and completely than I could have imagined.

It was soon winter again, or perhaps just another particularly cold summer, and to keep myself warm I made a practice
of shinning up the ivy at the side of the house into the old
man's bedroom and on to his bed. If there was a sound on
the stair he'd pull me under his blanket, which was an
experience I didn't relish, for he didn't wash very often and
if he did, he didn't wash very thoroughly. I don't know if he
was ill or anything, but he spent longer and longer in bed and
would sit up gazing out of the window and talk to himself, or
to me, or to the world at large. Sometimes he'd wake with a
start from his sleep and call for his wife, and then when he
saw the bed next to him, as she'd made it the day she died, he'd
pull himself up.

'Silly old crock, aren't I? She's gone, isn't she? Can't think
of anyone who isn't.'

Once when he called out his daughter rushed to the door,
huge curlers in her hair. I dived under the bed (into the old
man's half filled chamber, as it happens), but I caught a
glimpse of her and if she wasn't like the Gorgon's ugly sister
I don't know who is.

'What is it?' she demanded.

'What's what?'

'You were calling, didn't you hear? At the top of your
voice. You don't know what you're doing half the time. We'll
have to put you away if you go on like this.' And she slammed
the door.

'Put away,' I thought to myself, as I tried to shake myself
dry, what does she mean 'put away'? Is she going to take him
to the knacker's?

He was in a bad way, poor old chap, with one eye going and
the other one gone, and his memory flickering on and off like
a loose light-bulb, not that I minded for he'd bring me some

morsel to munch, always with the same words: 'There now, that should see you through till lunch time,' and ten minutes later he'd be round with another, and again: 'There now, that should see you through to lunch time,' but he could still get around on his own two feet, up and down the stairs, or for a longish walk in the park, and I'd sometimes trot along behind him.

He'd bring breadcrumbs and peanuts in his pocket to feed the birds. The birds would keep their distance while I was around, but squirrels would come out instead, Puffer among

them, who would give me apprehensive sidelong glances as they sat up on their hind legs and nibbled the nuts.

'They used to be red, the squirrels I mean,' he said; 'red

with a white dicky like yours, but they're all grey now – you don't see any red ones at all. Funny that. Did they change colour, or die out? Died out, I suppose . . . everybody's dying out. Haven't seen them in years, red squirrels. Of course it may be I'm going colour-blind.'

Usually after a longish walk he'd go upstairs and to bed, possibly because he was tired, but mainly, I suspect, to keep out of his daughter's way. He had got into the habit of rambling on to himself and whenever the Harridan was about she would tell him to shut up, and bed was about the only place where he could talk without interruption, which he often did, and, patient creature though I am, I too would have liked him to shut up, though he looked very sad when he did, with his white hair and his grey face and his red-rimmed, runny eyes. People look less sad when their jaws are going.

He didn't always talk to himself: more often than not he spoke to me.

'I like cats,' he said to me; 'they're the same as what they always were, cats. We had a cat when I was that big, my own private pet, a tabby, and other cats after that, and they were the same then as what they are now. They look the same. They eat the same sort of food and do the same sort of things. Everything else is changed, even squirrels, but not cats. They're the same as they always were. I like cats.' I almost grew to like him.

One day after he'd been out for about an hour or two, he came back and saw his daughter packing.

'You going somewhere?' he asked.

'No,' she said, 'but you are.'

'You mean for a bit in the country?'

'In the country, but more than a bit. You'll like it there, lovely grounds like a park. They'll look after you properly there. I can't.'

'What do you mean?'

'Looking after you and the house was a bit much for Mum, and it's getting to be a bit much for me. Besides, I want to take a job and earn some money and you can't be left on your own.'

'I don't mind being left on my own.'

'What, with your messy habits, breaking everything and tripping over everything and setting things on fire, and that smelly cat of yours? You'd have the place closed down as a health hazard. Besides, look at the house. It's falling to pieces. Have you the money to keep up repairs?'

'Repairs?'

'Repairs.'

'I've got a bob or two.'

'You'd need more than a bob or two, but in any case even if you had all the money in the world you couldn't be left on your own.'

'I don't mind being left on my own.'

'That's where I came in. Look, a friend's coming to take us in his car in another few minutes. See the place, if you don't like it you'll come back.'

Her friend was the red-faced man with the pock-marked neck. He arrived in a tiny, battered car and the old man was more pushed into it than helped into it. I don't know if he liked the other place or not, but he never came back.

The house seemed cold and empty when he was gone and food supplies – even rancid bacon rind – stopped. I began sniffing around dustbins and it's surprising what morsels they yield when you're hungry. I lost weight which made me a bit quicker. I was also a good bit hungrier and there's nothing like an empty stomach to put a bit of speed behind your tail. I managed to keep body and soul together by catching the occasional blackbird or sparrow but there were occasions that summer when I was so hungry that I was half tempted to have a nibble at Spike. I saw nothing of Brush or Pen or that lot for months on end and they had either forgotten me or were away for the summer. One day I managed to wing a plump pigeon about the size of a young duck, and after playing around with it for a bit I brought it back to the garage for a quiet feast, but the Harridan saw me, grabbed me and snatched the bird out of my mouth. I hadn't thought of her as part of the feathered-friends brigade, and she wasn't, for that night the bird was served up in a pie, which she shared with Pocked-

Neck, who, incidentally, had moved in as a permanent resident the day the Old Man was moved out.

There were times when there was nothing moving in the gardens and nothing edible in the bins, and I nearly starved.

One chilly morning, after I'd received nothing at all for two whole days and had been eating nettles and grass (which, whatever vegetarians may tell you, do *not* constitute a particularly nourishing diet), I had gone out to forage, determined to come back with something or die, when I noticed a large, well-fed rat. I had it by the neck in an instant and was about to administer the *coup de grâce* when it turned its head and I found myself looking into the terrified eyes of Puffer. I dropped him at once and he shot up a tree, to the uppermost branch, and remained there amid the swaying leaves, cursing me at the top of his voice. I was so famished that everything looked like a rat to me, but it seemed that poor Puffer had had an encounter with Genghis and came away minus his tail, and as if that hadn't been enough, he bumped into me and nearly came away minus his head.

I hurried on and some minutes later came across yet another rat, but before pouncing I looked closely to make sure it was not yet another squirrel. It was not, and I was upon it in a second, a trifle surprised at my own speed and agility. It fought back but it didn't take me long to subdue it and I was, so to speak, preparing it for the table when I became aware of the strong and unmistakable aroma of Public Enemy Number One, and in a moment Genghis stood before me. My normal instinct would have been to flee, but this time – again to my surprise – I stood my ground. Hunger makes heroes of us all. He was clearly taken aback by such chutzpah and inflated himself like a turkey-cock, and I did the same. He growled, I growled. He swished his tail, I swished mine. He yowled, I yowled. He moved slowly to the right (still inflated, tail still swishing), and I moved slowly to the right (still inflated, tail still swishing), and we must have looked as if we were doing a fandango. He growled again, I growled again: he yowled again, I yowled again. This went on for some time, but he got bored first and, after giving me a look which seemed to say,

'I'll let you off this time but don't let me find you here again,' he moved off. I was so elated by the incident that I forgot my hunger. I had stood my ground against Genghis, and I danced around trying to assimilate the full significance of my triumph. Minutes later, my hunger pangs returned and I went to look for the bleeding rat. It was gone. I wasn't sure who took it, but I suspect that Genghis had secured by stealth what he had failed to obtain by terror.

If Genghis no longer blighted my life, the Harridan continued to do so, nor was Pocked-Neck particularly friendly.

I didn't like the way they took over the house, especially in the evening, when he'd settle into Eric's chair and she into Rita's in front of the television, and, watching them in those same two chairs looking oh so different from their previous occupants, I could almost cry. Sometimes, without even drawing the curtains, she'd come over to his chair and settle on his knee and he'd put his hairy arms round her, and they'd sit cheek to cheek. A romantic sight it may have been, but lovely it wasn't.

She was out most of the day doing I don't know what, and he stayed at home painting this and mending that and pulling out old shelves and putting in new ones and generally pulling the place inside out. I suppose it looked cleaner and brighter, but I preferred the place as it was, and in any case I hated the smell of fresh paint. Not that I saw all that much of the house, for if I was ever about he'd try and kick me, or throw something at me, and as a rule I kept my distance. A cat, however, is a creature of habit, and I would shin up the ivy at the side of the house, in through the bedroom window and on to the old man's bed. On one such visit I landed plump on top of Pocked-Neck, who grabbed me by the scruff of the neck and threw me straight out of the window. I managed to grab hold of the ivy to break my fall, otherwise my story would have stopped short at this point.

Even that experience did not break me of my habit, though I did move with somewhat greater circumspection. One day I had nipped in through the window when I heard a sound on the landing and I dived under the bed (which, happily, was by now free of chambers). A pair of heavy feet entered, the window was pulled shut. Fortunately the door was left open and I was able to move about the house, but I couldn't move out. All the windows and doors were shut, locked, bolted, and there was no one in the house but myself. I was a prisoner.

I presumed the love-birds would be back in the evening, but the sun set and darkness came and there was no sign or sight of them and I fell asleep on the newly upholstered couch in the front room too hungry and tired to worry if I was caught or not. In any case I was on the ground floor, so that if I was thrown out of a window I wouldn't have far to fall.

I woke, I don't know how long later, aching with hunger and I set about sniffing in every corner, trying every crack, every window and every door in the house to see if there was an opening, but there was none, and I began searching for food instead. Before they had thrown the old man out one could pounce on the occasional mouse stirring about the place, but they had cleaned the place up and of mice there were none. I began scratching frantically at cupboards. The first one I opened was full of tins and I tried to bite or scratch them open. Several came clattering down to the floor but none broke open. In another cupboard I found several boxes of eggs, and while I was trying to bite through one it fell to the floor and there were smashed eggs everywhere. I sniffed them with little enthusiasm but beggars can't be choosers and for the first and, I hope, the last time in my life I had myself a meal of eggs. The whites were tasteless, but the yellows weren't too bad, even though they tasted of floor polish, and I must have gone through about a dozen of them before I felt I had had enough. When I looked up from my repast, dawn was beginning to break. The kitchen, by then, was not quite the spotless room she had left. There were tins, egg-boxes and eggshells all over the place and the floor was awash with egg-whites which had begun to harden, and I could hardly walk without slithering and everywhere I went I left a neat pattern of paw-marks edged with yellow. It was all rather pretty, if you like that sort of thing. I didn't imagine that she would like it particularly, and there would be hell to pay when she got back, but there was no hell worse than hunger and I settled myself in the corner of an armchair and fell asleep. I was wakened, I don't know how long later, by violent stomach cramp. I quickly rushed to the kitchen to make my way out into the garden and only then remembered that I was a prisoner, but still I tried every possible opening – and a few impossible ones – before reconciling myself to my fate and I sought out an obscure corner of the lounge, between the couch and the bay window, and did what anyone else in my position would have done including, I dare say, the Harridan. I should have liked to find a bit of soil or some dead leaves to cover it with, but there was nothing, and I had to leave it there, hoping that no one would notice. A minute later I had to go to the same place to do the same thing, and the minute

thereafter once more. I was not at all well. It was a blazing hot day and the garden was full of birds, as if they knew I was a prisoner inside the house and had come out in force to mock me – pigeons, sea-gulls, blackbirds, ravens, crows, sparrows, swallows, starlings, robins, bluetits, a bleeding convention. My tail fluffed up and thumped from side to side but the rest of me felt inert, with no appetite to chase anyone or eat anyone or anything. On the contrary, my stomach began to heave and I emptied my innards on to the kitchen floor and slunk away into a cool, dark corner to sleep and, if possible, to die.

I was awakened maybe an hour later, or maybe a day, by a loud scream. I looked up from my corner and there she was standing by the open door with her mouth open and her hands to her face. Pocked-Neck appeared a minute later, and all he could say was: 'Christ, the pong!'

I thought I had no strength left, but as soon as I heard her I rose to my feet and shot out between them, and into the garden like a streak, and kept my distance for the rest of the day.

Once in the open I felt much better and soon recovered my appetite. The birds, needless to say, had by then flown, and I made my way to Zombie's house and was relieved to see some signs of life. I found the children playing in the back garden. Pen was the first to see me but she regarded me with interest rather than enthusiasm.

'Oh look,' she said, 'that cat there, it's just like Bell.'

'Bell isn't that thin,' said Son-of-Zombie.

'Bell isn't that thin,' echoed his brother.

'I didn't say it was Bell,' said Pen, 'but it's got the same colouring, the same white dicky, the same white . . .' She bent down to have a closer look. 'You know I think it *is* Bell.'

'It isn't.'

'It is.'

At which point Brush-in-hand appeared with brush in hand.

'My God,' she said, 'it's Bell.'

'It isn't.'

'Of course it is.'

'Bell isn't that thin.'

'It wasn't, but they've starved it. Poor pussy.'

'Don't touch it,' said Pen, 'it looks as if it's full of fleas. What have they done to you, poor thing?'

Let's have an end to commiseration, I thought to myself, and let's see some food, at which Son-of-Zombie brought out something on a plate. I didn't even look to see what it was but gobbled it up. They then brought some milk.

'Look, he looks better already,' said Pen. I felt better already.

Zombie came out and stroked me, Scragends chucked me under the chin and Clarence, Puffer and Spike came by to see how I was doing. It was like a family reunion.

I had a sleep after my repast and then, without thinking, wandered down the road not because I had any business down the road but because it was the thing I normally did after a meal and a sleep. My exile, the hard times, the hunger, all seemed like a bad dream. I was back among non-enemies. And so I moved on, musing pleasantly, when suddenly a heavy hand fell upon me, pulling my skin so tight that my eyes almost popped out of my head and I was lifted by the scruff of the neck. I couldn't see who it was, but the grip was a distinctly unfriendly one. I peered round slowly and painfully, like a rusty weather-vane and found myself face to face with Pocked-Neck. It was the first time I had seen him in close-up and I found his face even less attractive than his neck. His eyes were bloodshot, he had bad teeth and his breath smelt. Then, as he held me in one hand, he picked up a trowel and struck me across the head with the other. I was nearly stunned, but the very pain somehow gave me new strength. I suddenly wrenched myself free and even as I was in the air I struck out with all twenty claws, landed on my feet, shot through a hedge and dived into the first hiding-place I could find, which happened to be a van. I must have made my mark. In fact I was sure I had for he filled the air with shouts and curses and there was some blood on my forepaws, which I contemplated with warm satisfaction before licking them clean. I heard him rampaging about the place and threatening to do things to me I wouldn't even have wished on his lady friend.

'I'll kill the bloody beast,' he kept screaming. 'I'll bash its head in, I'll tear it to pieces, I'll skin it alive.' And they say the British are animal lovers. I was anxious to get out for I am nervous of being cooped up in a confined space, but for the time being I felt it wise to keep what they call a low profile and I remained there till the commotion subsided. I must have fallen asleep then for I was wakened by a swaying motion and before I knew what was happening the van was roaring down the road with me in the back in a state of utter petrification.

I don't really ask much of life but if there is one thing I insist on it is that terra firma should be, well, firma, and though I don't mind moving I hate being moved, so that even the thought of being perched on a swaying branch is enough to send me into a tizzy. I once, and only once, found myself in a moving vehicle and dived out of the open window before it got far and was nearly cut down by oncoming traffic. This time there was no window open, but what turned me to stone was the face of the driver which I could glimpse vaguely in the driving mirror, and which was unmistakeable – it was the Harridan. I never knew that she could drive, or that she drove a van. That may have been what she did for a living. She wasn't as violent as her gentleman friend, but neither was she the soul of sweetness and if she found me there at the back, my life would turn out to be nasty and short. In the meantime the doors were shut, the windows were shut and there was nothing I could do except lie low and wait.

She must have driven for about an hour before turning up a country lane and then up a winding, gravelled drive and finally pulling up outside a vast edifice, with towers and battlements, a stately home of some sort which looked as if it had known better times. Then as she opened the door to get out I jumped on to her shoulder and out into freedom. I took her completely unaware for she gave a scream, as if the Angel of Death had set upon her (which I wish it had), and she danced round in circles as if trying to shake it off. I, in the meantime, had dived through a bush and she couldn't have seen me at all.

Back in the parish Zombie's children had heard Pocked-Neck fill the air with threats against my person and they went rushing to their father to demand that he call the police, the fire brigade, the Chief Rabbi, the RSPCA.

'Do something,' Pen insisted, 'and quick.'

'Am I Belshazzar's keeper?' he asked.

'Yes,' they retorted.

'He's been starved,' said Brush, 'and if you don't come with us to see what's happening they may kill him.'

'Nothing doing,' he said and returned to doing nothing.

Scragends, I need hardly add, was no more sympathetic and the children rushed down the road on their own, where they found Clarence running backwards and forwards and looking agitated in the extreme. He had seen me being driven off in

the van and had followed the vehicle for some distance barking at the top of his voice, but had lost it in heavy traffic. Now followed by the children, he resumed the trail, over one road, along another, and then a third and on into the fields, at which point Brush stopped.

'It's like looking for a needle in a haystack and it's getting dark,' she said. 'We'd better get back.'

'But he may kill him,' said Son-of-Zombie. 'He looked very cruel, that man.'

'But we'll never find him in the dark,' said Pen, 'and anyway it looks as if Clarence has lost the trail.'

'We'd better go back,' said Brush; 'it's dark already and we'll be late for super.'

'But what about Bell?' asked Son-of-Zombie.

'We'll have to come back and look for him tomorrow.'

'No,' he said, 'let's look for him now. We may lose him.' But what had happened was that they had lost themselves. They relied on Clarence to guide them home, but he too was lost (as he usually is). It was getting cold, they were hungry and Angel began to cry.

When supper was ready, Scragends called out for the children, but they didn't appear.

'Will you tell them to come down for supper,' she shouted to Zombie, 'the soup's getting cold'

'Will you come down for supper,' Zombie shouted, 'the soup's getting cold.' But his voice echoed through the empty house. He went to their rooms but they weren't there. He looked in the front garden, the back garden, the attic, the garage, the garden shed, the wendy house; there was no sign of them.

'What do you mean, there's no sign of them?' said Scragends.

'They've vanished.'

She took off her apron and they both searched again. They tried the streets, their neighbours. No one had seen them. They went down to the Harridan. The house was locked and in darkness. They tried the next street and found Clarence's master meandering along the pavement.

'M'dog,' he said, 'have you seen m'dog? He's gone, m'dog. Vanished.'

'Could this be some sort of game they're playing?' said Zombie.

'What sort of game?' asked Scragends.

'Hide and seek,'

'I'm going to the police.'

The police appeared within minutes, two large policemen in a small car.

'Everyone seems to be vanishing this evening,' said one of them. 'We've just had an old drunk calling us about his lost dog.'

At which Zombie had an idea (he sometimes does).

'It occurs to me that the dog and the kids could have gone off together. They were all friendly with Belshazzar.'

'With who?' asked the policeman.

'With the cat, and they were worried about the cat and they may have gone off to look for it.'

'You want us to find the cat as well?' said the policeman.

'If we find the cat we'll find the children and the dog, or vice versa,' said Zombie.

And when the police began knocking on doors people did remember seeing a huge black dog bounding down the street in full cry. Funny how people will remember dogs, but not children or cats. Anyway, this gave the police the clue they needed and by midnight the children were safely in bed. I wish I could have said the same for myself.

CHAPTER 5

I stayed in the hedge for a minute or two till the Harridan was out of sight, and might have remained there for much longer, for I felt oddly insecure and was not in the mood to venture out among humans, but for the smell of food. It could not have been all that long since my last meal, but the smell of food disposes me readily for my next one, and I followed the odour along a narrow path, down through an open basement window and along the cold stone floor of what seemed to be an endless corridor and there became aware of other, less pleasant smells, floor polish and disinfectant. I climbed up a spiral staircase and trotted along a broad corridor with parquet flooring, somehow becoming more venturesome with each step. There was an open door with a green curtain across it. I put my head round the curtain, and quickly pulled it back. The Harridan was there talking to someone propped up in bed. She was pulling plums and grapes out of a bag and was trying to induce him to eat them.

'Go on, have one dad,' she kept saying. 'It'll do you good.'

Dad. I took a peek round the curtain, and there was Eric, not quite large as life, for he was shrivelled a bit, poor fellow. His face was sunken and gaunt, his nose seemed longer, and the bags under his eyes were large enough to take his laundry, but I was surprised to see him at all, for I thought she had taken him to the knacker's. She bent over to straighten his pillow.

'Are you happy here, Dad?' she asked.

I didn't hear his reply, but he didn't look like a picture of happiness.

I walked back along the corridor, put my head round another door and found myself in a huge kitchen with tiled walls, steel tables, steel sinks and fish ready for the pot laid out in a row. I jumped up, grabbed a fish and fled with the creature dangling down both sides of my jaws, almost tripping as I went, and ate it quietly in the shrubbery. I then had a drink from a stream and retired once again to the shelter of the shrubbery. This I decided, would be my home, until further notice, and I remained there foraging with immunity, grabbing what I could and vanishing at the first sign of movement. I was enjoying life but for the fact that my head was for some reason becoming larger and heavier and I was losing my fur about my neck and shoulders.

Then the weather changed. It became cold and wet and I yearned for a bit of warmth, and one afternoon I went into one of the rooms and found it full of old men huddled in front of a large television set, with one figure in a corner gazing into space. It was Eric. He wasn't stirring at all, but when he saw me slinking along by the radiators his good eye lit up.

'It isn't Bell, is it?' he said. His legs were covered with a rug and I jumped on to his lap.

'Ee you look as if you've come upon hard times,' he said stroking me the wrong way up.

I felt like retorting: 'You look as if you've seen better days yourself.'

At that moment someone smelling of carbolic and starch entered and all the old men in the room straightened up. Eric brushed me from his lap as if I was crumbs and I dived under a curtain.

'Time gentlemen please,' she said. 'It's long past your bedtime.' The television was switched off and there was a grunting and shuffling and clattering of sticks as the company rose and made their way to their rooms. I followed Eric, darting now behind a curtain, now behind a pillar, now behind a radiator. Movement wasn't easy, because the floors were highly polished and it was a miracle none of the old crocks went on their necks. The rooms in fact turned out to be tiny cubicles, a bed, a chair and a small table, and you could hear everything that went on in the next cubicle and, what was worse, smelt everything, and there was much groaning and spluttering and farting as the company settled down to sleep. Eric had a jam jar with three or four dead flowers in it, a glass full of teeth and a framed photograph of Rita with a cat in her lap which must have been taken shortly before she died, for I was the cat. I recognised myself from the colouring, but otherwise I felt like a poor cousin of that overblown, pampered pile of fluff.

'It was better back home, wasn't it?' said Eric.

'Depends in whose company,' I thought.

He took a spoonful of one medicine, then a mouthful of another and a capsule and a pill and settled back to sleep and I also was beginning to drop off when the curtain was suddenly pulled aside and I dived under his bed and landed in his chamber. Quite like old times.

I was quite well off for, apart from things I pinched, old Eric was always pinching something for me (though I suspect he half starved himself in the process), but it was a cat and mouse existence – with me in the role of mouse. Pets (insofar as I was one) were definitely not admitted and whenever I was caught sight of I was chased by a whole army of angry-looking people brandishing brooms, sticks and kitchen utensils.

There was a day in the week – Sunday I think – when the

place was crowded with visitors and I gave it a wide berth.

One day, however, I noticed a familiar figure among the visitors, Scragends, and to my surprise I was almost glad to see her. Eric was unwell that day and she came up to his room.

'I was passing,' she said, 'so I thought I'd look in to see how you were. Do you get a lot of visitors?'

'Visitors?'

'Do you get a lot of visitors?'

'No, not a lot. There's the wife of course, but she's dead, and my brother, he's dead – he's been dead for a very long time, my brother. Did you know him?'

'No, I'm afraid not.'

'No, he's been dead for longer than he's been alive come to think of it. He was a builder, you know, and was fixing a lintel. He was a good builder, but lintels was his weak point, and one day – seems like yesterday, but it was over fifty years ago. Yes, he's dead. Then there's my wife, you knew my wife . . .?'

'Very well.'

'Nearly two years since she died. Things haven't been the same since. Then there's me daughter – she's not dead – but she's working you see, so she can't make it often. You know my daughter?'

'Yes, we've met.'

'She's got a young man, you know. They're waiting to marry. In fact they'd have married last week, or was it last month, I can't remember now, only I was taken poorly and she had to drop everything and rush over here. I nearly moved on, in fact I thought I had and when I got back here there was someone else in me bed – trying on my teeth, if you please. You know what keeps me going?'

'No.'

'I don't myself. I sometimes feel so bad of an evening that I say to myself I'll be seeing Rita before the night's out, but I open my eyes and here I'm back where I was. Two years nearly since she died. Seems like yesterday.'

'Still you've got your daughter's wedding to look forward to.'

'What's that?'

'Your daughter's wedding.'

'My daughter?'

'Yes.'

'What about her?'

'She's getting married.'

'Did she tell you that? Yes, she's got a young man. I don't fancy him much, I'm surprised she does. I gave her a good education, my daughter, but she's done nothing with it. His people aren't up to much, as a matter of fact he's got none. I mean you'd think he'd have some sort of family – he's English after all – but he's got none. Doesn't say much for him does it? But I wouldn't interfere. Wouldn't help much if I did. Young people do as they like these days. As a matter of fact they should have got married last month, or was it last week, I can't remember now, but I was taken poorly. I nearly moved on. People do you know, they're very quiet about it, but they do. They just pull those curtains round and the next thing you know is you've got a new neighbour.'

'But I must say you're looking very cheerful.'

'Very what?'

'Cheerful.'

'Well, yes, as long as I've got me health – it's what counts isn't it? And, as I said, my daughter comes every now and again.'

'She's a good daughter, isn't she?'

'A good what?'

'Daughter.'

'Well, yes, ever since I've left home she has been, but she can't come too often, she's working you see. And then there's . . . ' He looked about him. 'Where is he? He usually likes to sit on top of the bed when no one's about.'

At which point I felt it safe to come out of hiding. I expected a smile, but instead encountered something like a grimace and she seemed to recoil.

'Who's that?'

'What's that?'

'Who's that?'

'Don't you recognise him?'

'It isn't Bell, is it?'

'Right first time, lost a bit of weight round his flanks – see, you can count his ribs – but he's put it on round his head, and he's beginning to moult.'

'That isn't moulting. His fur's coming away. He doesn't look at all well to me.'

'He doesn't, does he? I was thinking of having a word with the doctor.'

'Are you sure it's nothing infectious?'

'Nothing what?'

'Infectious.'

'Well, I don't suppose he could have anything which could do me harm, not at my age. In any case I've had everything going twice over.'

'Poor Bell.' She stroked me with a somewhat hesitating hand. 'He looks as if he might have myxomatosis.'

'He might, but I've probably had it myself, so there's no harm done.'

'Are you allowed to keep cats?'

'Cats? No, no pets at all, no women, nothing like that. It's the rules you see. Chap in the next cubicle tried to smuggle in his budgerigar. Got stifled in his pocket. Bell here had what was left.'

She stayed for about an hour and stroked me again before she left, something she had never done in my plush, strokable years, and I followed her out of the building and into the garden. I don't know what I expected from her. Pussy Pats? Did I hope she might take me back to Brush, Pen and the others? I wouldn't have minded, but she got into her car and was off, without another word.

Later in the day, when the visitors had left and the place was settling down to sleep, I made my furtive way back to Eric's cubicle, hoping to have some of the warm milk which was brought to his bed side every night, but he wasn't there. I presumed he had gone to the toilet and I got on to his bed and waited – a fatal thing to do. I must have fallen asleep and when I woke I found myself in the grip of someone I couldn't see but who was wearing rubber gloves and hurrying me down the corridor and down, down, down into a cellar. It turned out to be the boiler room and a man with sweaty arms and a grubby vest was stoking the furnace.

'I've got the brute,' said my captor.

'Here,' said the stoker, 'throw him right in,' and he opened the furnace door, at which I gave a sudden twist, wrenched myself free and sped up the stairs and out into the night.

A few days passed before I had the nerve to get back to Eric's cubicle, but I was anxious to see if he was all right, and in any case I was hungry for a bit of milk. I moved very carefully, darting in and out of the shadows, remaining motionless whenever someone appeared, and I finally made it to his bed and noticed, with relief, that he was back. A glass of milk was cooling beside him, but he was fast asleep. I jumped up to help myself and while doing so noticed that the photo beside him was not of Rita and me but of a young woman with an infant on her lap. I looked around to see if I was in the right cubicle. It was the first one by the door, and there were the same dead flowers (now deader than ever) in the same jam jar, and it smelt like Eric, but as I had a closer look at his face I saw that it wasn't him.

Eric had been moved. I finally found him in another part of the building, not in a cubicle but in a hospital ward with about a dozen beds on each side. He was fast asleep with his mouth open, and a plastic tube attached to his arm. Nearly all the men in the ward looked alike and most of them had tubes going in at one end and coming out at another and I only recognised him by his bedside photo.

It had been risky getting into the ward and it would have been even riskier getting out, for there were people coming and going, and I remained motionless under the bed (no chamber there, I suppose he didn't need one with all those tubes) though I was nearly asphyxiated by the smell of floor polish. Then I was startled by movement round his bed, first one pair of feet, then two pairs and the sound of anxious voices, then perhaps half a dozen pairs and a lot of commotion in the bed so that I was afraid it might collapse on top of me. Then the commotion stopped, the feet moved away, and all was quiet. When I put my head out, the bed was empty and the picture had been removed, though they had left his teeth behind. Eric was dead and, rather oddly, I felt more sorry for myself than for him.

The funeral was the next day, a very small affair, with the Harridan and her beloved in one car and perhaps half a dozen neighbours in another two cars, including Zombie, looking a trifle odd in a black bowler hat.

I had been keeping my distance as the cars assembled, but he noticed me and came towards me and I wondered whether to run or not. I stayed my ground and he reached out a gloved hand, picked me up, pulled a face and put me down. He was back a few hours later with Brush, Pen and the rest and they scooped me up in a basket and took me home.

They first called the vet to look me over, and he held me up to his face, shaking his head all the while, as if to say, 'There's nothing I can do for him,' and threw me into a basket and took me off in his car.

This was me, I took it, heading for the last round-up, for my second and final operation. I was about to be put to sleep, but, if so, it was a drawn-out process. He began with a series of injections, which did not put me to sleep, but made me feel odd and dizzy, or rather drunk, for I kept jumping from heights and tried to take off with wings flapping, and of course landed on my face. Then came great white pills, which he literally rammed down my throat. It was days before I saw anything as substantial as food, but I will admit that after a few days I felt the better for the treatment and after a fortnight I was brought back home, with all my bald patches covered with a new growth of hair and all of my sores healed, and my head felt so light that I wasn't quite sure it was there. After a further fortnight I was, as someone observed, 'in showroom condition'.

And so it was back to things as they were, except that they aren't. Brush-in-hand seems to have no time for me at all, and Pen-in-hand no longer tries to draw bow-ties on my dicky. Son-of-Zombie dangles bits of string in front of me and complains that Bell doesn't like playing any more and Angel dangles strings in front of me and makes the same complaint. He also rolls balls over to me and marbles and the most he can get out of me is a look of majestic disdain. Next door Sha and She have grown so vast and obese and motionless that they look like stuffed animals, which is what perhaps they were. I feel a little like one myself. The garden is alive with birds of all shapes and sizes, among them an escaped canary, and they peck away at breadcrumbs in my very shadow, but I feel disinclined to chase. Zombie, who used to doze in the afternoon, has taken to dozing in the morning and I don't get the impression that he loses too much sleep at night either. Spike has vanished (they say he floated off on a cloud of fleas), Clarence has been castrated, Genghis has been run over and stuffed. Scragends has mellowed, though she still serves

Pussy Pats and as a matter of fact I like them; perhaps I always did.

Plus c'est la même chose, plus ça change. The more things stay the same, the more they change.